P9-DGV-873

BOOKS BY MILDRED D. TAYLOR

The Friendship
The Gold Cadillac
Let the Circle Be Unbroken
Mississippi Bridge
The Road to Memphis
Roll of Thunder, Hear My Cry
Song of the Trees
The Well

The
FRIENDSHIP

MILDRED D. TAYLOR

Pictures by Max Ginsburg

PUFFIN BOOKS

PUFFIN BOOKS
Published by the Penguin Group
Penguin Putnam Inc., 375 Hudson Street, New York, New York 10014, U.S.A.
Penguin Books Ltd, 27 Wrights Lane, London W8 5TZ, England
Penguin Books Australia Ltd, Ringwood, Victoria, Australia
Penguin Books Canada Ltd, 10 Alcorn Avenue, Toronto, Ontario, Canada M4V 3B2
Penguin Books (N.Z.) Ltd, 182-190 Wairau Road, Auckland 10, New Zealand

Penguin Books Ltd, Registered Offices: Harmondsworth, Middlesex, England

First published in the United States of America by Dial Books for Young Readers, 1987
Published in Puffin Books, 1998

5 7 9 10 8 6

THE LIBRARY OF CONGRESS HAS CATALOGED THE DIAL EDITION AS FOLLOWS:
Taylor, Mildred D. The friendship.
Summary: Four children witness a confrontation between an elderly black
man and a white storekeeper in rural Mississippi in the 1930s.
[1. Afro-Americans—Fiction. 2. Southern states—Race relations—Fiction.
3. Race relations—Fiction. 4. Prejudices—Fiction.] I. Ginsburg, Max, ill.
II. Title.
PZ7.T21723Fr 1987 [Fic] 86-29309
ISBN 0-8037-0417-8   ISBN 0-8037-0418-6 (lib. bdg.)

Puffin Books ISBN 0-14-038964-4

Printed in the United States of America

In memory of my father, the storyteller

"Now don't y'all go touchin' nothin'," Stacey warned as we stepped onto the porch of the Wallace store. Christopher-John, Little Man, and I readily agreed to that. After all, we weren't even supposed to be up here. "And Cassie," he added, "don't you say nothin'."

"Now, boy, what I'm gonna say?" I cried, indignant that he should single me out.

"Just mind my words, hear? Now come on." Stacey started for the door, then stepped back as Jeremy Simms, a blond sad-eyed boy, came out. Looking out from under the big straw hat he was wearing, he glanced somewhat shyly at us, then gave a nod. We took a moment and nodded back. At first I thought Jeremy was going to say something. He looked as if he wanted to, but then he walked on past and went slowly down the steps. We all watched him. He got as far as the corner of the porch and looked back. The boys and I turned and went into the store.

Once inside we stood in the entrance a moment, somewhat hesitant now about being here. At the back counter, two of the storekeepers, Thurston and Dewberry Wallace, were stocking shelves. They glanced over, then paid us no further attention. I didn't much like them. Mama and Papa didn't much like them either. They didn't much like any of the Wallaces and that included Dewberry and Thurston's brother, Kaleb, and their father, John. They said the Wallaces didn't treat our folks right and it was best to stay clear of them. Because of that they didn't come up to this store to shop and we weren't supposed to be coming up here either.

We all knew that. But today as we had walked the red road toward home, Aunt Callie Jackson, who wasn't really our aunt but whom everybody called that because she was so old, had hollered to us from her front porch and said she had the headache bad. She said her nephew Joe was gone off somewhere and she had nobody to send to the store for head medicine. We couldn't say no to her, not to Aunt Callie. So despite Mama's and Papa's warnings about this Wallace place, we had taken it upon ourselves to come anyway. Stacey had said they would understand and after a moment's thought had added that if they didn't he would take the blame and that had settled it. After all, he was twelve with three years on me, so I made no objection about the thing. Christopher-John and Little Man, younger still, nodded agreement and that was that.

"Now mind what I said," Stacey warned us again, then headed for the back counter and the Wallaces. Christopher-John, Little Man, and I remained by the front door looking the store over; it was our first time in the place. The store was small, not nearly as large as it had looked from the outside peeping in. Farm supplies and household and food goods were sparsely displayed on the shelves and counters and the floor space too, while on the walls were plastered posters of a man called Roosevelt. In the center of the store was a potbellied stove, and near it a table and some chairs. But nobody was sitting there. In fact, there were no other customers in the store.

Our eyes roamed over it all with little interest; then we spotted the three large jars of candy on one of the counters. One was filled with lemon drops, another with licorice, and a third with candy canes. Christopher-John, who was seven, round, and had himself a mighty sweet tooth, glanced around at Little Man and me, grinning. Then he walked over to the candy jars for a closer look. There he stood staring at them with a hungry longing even though he knew good and well there would be no candy for him this day. There never was for any of us except at Christmastime. Little Man started to follow him, but then something else caught his eye. Something gleaming and shining. Belt buckles and lockets, cuff links, and tie clips in a glass case.

As soon as Little Man saw them, he forgot about the jars of candy and strutted right over. Little Man loved shiny new things.

Not interested in drooling over candy I knew I couldn't have, or shiny new things either, I went on to the back and stood with Stacey. Since the Wallaces were taking their own good time about serving us, I busied myself studying a brand-new 1933 catalog that lay open on the counter. Finally, Dewberry asked what we wanted. Stacey was about to tell him, but before he could, Dewberry's eyes suddenly widened and he slapped the rag he was holding against the counter and hollered, "Get them filthy hands off-a-there!"

Stacey and I turned to see who he was yelling at. So did Christopher-John. Then we saw Little Man. Excited by the lure of all those shiny new things, Little Man had forgotten Stacey's warning. Standing on tiptoe, he was bracing himself with both hands against the top of the glass counter for a better look inside. Now he glanced around. He found Dewberry's eyes on him and snatched his hands away. He hid them behind his back.

Dewberry, a full-grown man, stared down at Little Man. Little Man, only six, looked up. "Now I'm gonna hafta clean that glass again," snapped Dewberry, "seeing you done put them dirty hands-a yours all over it!"

"My hands ain't dirty," Little Man calmly informed him. He seemed happy that he could set Dewberry's mind to rest if that was all that was bothering him. Little Man pulled his hands from behind his back and inspected them. He turned his hands inward. He turned them outward. Then he held them up for Dewberry to see. "They clean!" he said. "They ain't dirty! They clean!"

Dewberry came from around the corner. "Boy, you disputin' my word? Just look at ya! Skin's black as dirt. Could put seeds on ya and have 'em growin' in no time!"

Thurston Wallace laughed and tossed his brother an ax from one of the shelves. "Best chop them hands off, Dew, they that filthy!"

Little Man's eyes widened at the sight of the ax. He slapped his hands behind himself again and backed away. Stacey hurried over and put an arm around him. Keeping

eyes on the Wallaces, he brought Little Man back to stand with us. Thurston and Dewberry laughed.

We got Aunt Callie's head medicine and hurried out. As we reached the steps we ran into Mr. Tom Bee carrying a fishing pole and two strings of fish. Mr. Tom Bee was an elderly, toothless man who had a bit of sharecropping land over on the Granger Plantation. But Mr. Tom Bee didn't do much farming these days. Instead he spent most of his days fishing. Mr. Tom Bee loved to fish. "Well, now," he said, coming up the steps, "where y'all younguns headed to?"

Stacey nodded toward the crossroads. "Over to Aunt Callie's, then on home."

"Y'all hold on up a minute, I walk with ya. Got a mess-a fish for Aunt Callie. Jus' wants to drop off this here other string and get me some more-a my sardines. I loves fishin' cat, but I keeps me a taste for sardines!" he laughed.

Stacey watched him go into the store, then looked back to the road. There wasn't much to see. There was a lone gas pump in front of the store. There were two red roads that crossed each other, and a dark forest that loomed on the other three corners of the crossroads. That was all, yet Stacey was staring out intensely as if there were more to see. A troubled look was on his face and anger was in his eyes.

"You figure we best head on home?" I asked.

"Reckon we can wait, Mr. Tom Bee don't take too long," he said, then leaned moodily back against the post. I knew his moods and I knew this one had nothing to do with Mr. Tom Bee. So I let him be and sat down on the steps in the shade of the porch trying to escape some of the heat. It was miserably hot. But then it most days was in a Mississippi summer. Christopher-John sat down too, but not Little Man. He remained by the open doors staring into the store. Christopher-John noticed him there and immediately hopped back up again. Always sympathizing with other folks' feelings, he went over to Little Man and tried to comfort him. "Don'tcha worry now, Man," he said, patting his shoulder. "Don'tcha worry! We knows you ain't dirty!"

"That ain't what they said!" shrieked Little Man, his voice revealing the hurt he felt. Little Man took great pride in being clean.

Stacey turned to them. "Man, forget about what they said. You can't pay them no mind."

"But, St-Stacey! They said they could plant seeds on me!" he cried indignantly.

I looked back at him. "Ah, shoot, boy! You know they can't do no such-a thing!"

Skeptically Little Man looked to Stacey for affirmation.

Stacey nodded. "They can do plenty all right, but they can't do nothin' like that."

"But—but, Stacey, th-they s-said they was g-gonna c-cut off my hands. They done s-said they gonna do that c-cause they . . . they dirty!"

Stacey said nothing for a moment, then pulled from the post and went over to him. "They was jus' teasin' you, Man," he said softly, "that's all. They was jus' teasin'. Their way of funnin'."

"Wasn't nothin' 'bout it funny to me," I remarked, feeling Little Man's hurt.

Stacey's eyes met mine and I knew he was feeling the same. He brought Little Man back to the steps and the two of them sat down. Little Man, seemingly comforted with Stacey beside him, was silent now. But after a few moments he did a strange thing. He reached down and placed his hand flat to the dirt. He looked at his hand, looked at the dirt, then drew back again. Without a word, he folded his hands tightly together and held them very still in his lap.

I looked at the ground, then at him. "Now what was all that about?"

Little Man looked at me, his eyes deeply troubled. And once again, Stacey said, "Forget it, Man, forget it."

Little Man said nothing, but I could tell he wasn't forgetting anything. I stared down at the dirt. I wasn't forgetting either.

" 'Ey, y'all."

We turned. Jeremy Simms was standing at the corner of the porch.

"Boy, I thought you was gone!" I said.

Stacey nudged me to be quiet, but didn't say anything to Jeremy himself. Jeremy bit at his lip, his face reddening. Rubbing one bare foot against the other, he pushed his hands deep into his overall pockets. "C-come up here to wait on my pa and R.W. and Melvin," he explained. "Got a load to pick up. Been waiting a good while now."

Stacey nodded. There wasn't anything to say to that. Jeremy seemed to understand there was nothing to say. A fly buzzed near his face. He brushed it away, looked out at the crossroads, then sat down at the end of the porch and leaned against a post facing us. He pulled one leg up toward his chest and left the other leg dangling over the side of the porch. He glanced at us, looked out at the cross-roads, then back at us again. "Y'all . . . y'all been doin' a lotta fishin' here lately?"

Stacey glanced over. "Fish when we can."

"Over on the Rosa Lee?"

Stacey nodded his answer.

"I fish over there sometimes. . . . "

"Most folks do. . . . " said Stacey.

Jeremy was silent a moment as if thinking on what he should say next. "Y'all . . . y'all spect to be goin' fishin' again anyways soon?"

Stacey shook his head. "Cotton time's here. Got too much work to do now for much fishin'."

"Yeah, me too I reckon. . . ."

Jeremy looked away once more and was quiet once more. I watched him, trying to figure him out. The boy was a mighty puzzlement to me, the way he was always talking friendly to us. I didn't understand it. He was white.

Stacey saw me staring and shook his head, letting me know I shouldn't be doing it. So I stopped. After that we all just sat there in the muggy midday heat listening to the sounds of bees and flies and cawing blackbirds and kept our silence. Then we heard voices rising inside the store and turned to look. Mr. Tom Bee, the string of fish and the fishing pole still in his hand, was standing before the counter listening to Dewberry.

"Now look here, old uncle," said Dewberry, "I told you three times my daddy's busy! You tell me what you want or get on outa here. I ain't got all day to fool with you."

Mr. Tom Bee was a slightly built man, and that along with his age made him look somewhat frail, and especially so as he faced the much younger Dewberry. But that look of frailty didn't keep him from speaking his mind. There was a sharp-edged stubbornness to Mr. Tom Bee. His eyes ran over both Dewberry and Thurston and he snapped: "Give me some-a them sardines! Needs me four cans!"

Dewberry leaned across the counter. "You already got plenty-a charges, Tom. You don't need no sardines. Ya stinkin' of fish as it is."

I nudged Stacey. "Now how he know what Mr. Tom Bee need?"

Stacey told me to hush.

"Well, shoot! Mr. Tom Bee been grown more years than 'bout anybody 'round here! He oughta know what he need!"

"Cassie, I said hush!" Stacey glanced back toward the store as if afraid somebody inside might have heard. Then he glanced over at Jeremy, who bit his lower lip and looked away again as if he had heard nothing at all.

Saying nothing else, Stacey looked back at the crossroads. I cut my eyes at him, then sighed. I was tired of always having to watch my mouth whenever white folks were around. Wishing Mr. Tom Bee would get his stuff and come on, I got up and crossed the porch to the doorway. It was then I saw that Christopher-John had eased back inside and was again staring up at the candy jars. I started to tell Stacey that Christopher-John was in the store, then realized Mr. Tom Bee had noticed him too. Seeing Christopher-John standing there, Mr. Tom Bee pointed to the candy and said to Dewberry, "An' you can jus' give me some-a them candy canes there too."

"Don't need no candy canes neither, Tom," decided Dewberry. "Got no teeth to chew 'em with."

Mr. Tom Bee stood his ground. "Y'all can't get them sardines and that candy for me, y'all go get y'alls daddy and let him get it! Where John anyway?" he demanded. "He give me what I ask for, you sorry boys won't!"

Suddenly the store went quiet. I could feel something was wrong. Stacey got up. I looked at him. We both knew this name business was a touchy thing. I didn't really understand why, but it was. White folks took it seriously.

Mighty seriously. They took it seriously to call every grown black person straight out by their first name without placing a "mister" or a "missus" or a "miss" anywhere. White folks, young and old, called Mama and Papa straight out by their first names. They called Big Ma by her first name or they sometimes called her aunty because she was in her sixties now and that was their way of showing her age some respect, though Big Ma said she didn't need that kind of respect. She wasn't *their* aunty. They took seriously too the way we addressed them. All the white grown folks I knew expected to be addressed proper with that "mister" and "missus" sounding loud ahead of their names. No, I didn't understand it. But I understood enough to know Mr. Tom Bee could be in trouble standing up in this store calling Dewberry and Thurston's father John straight out.

Jeremy glanced from the store to us, watching, his lips pressed tight. I could tell he understood the seriousness of names too. Stacey moved toward me. It was then he saw Christopher-John inside the store. He bit his lip nervously, as if trying to decide if he should bring attention to Christopher-John by going in to get him. I think the quiet made him wait.

Dewberry pointed a warning finger at Mr. Tom Bee. "Old nigger," he said, "don't you never in this life speak to me that way again. And don't you never stand up there with yo' black face and speak of my daddy or any other white man without the proper respect. You might be of a forgetful mind at yo' age, but you forgettin' the wrong thing when you forgettin' who you are. A nigger, nothin' but a nigger. You may be old, Tom, but you ain't too old to teach and you ain't too old to whip!"

My breath caught and I shivered. It was such a little thing, I figured, this thing about a name. I just couldn't understand it. I just couldn't understand it at all.

The back door to the store slammed and a man appeared in the doorway. He was average-built and looked to be somewhere in his fifties. The man was John Wallace, Dewberry and Thurston's father. He looked at Mr. Tom Bee, then motioned to his sons. "I take care-a this," he said.

Mr. Tom Bee grinned. "Well, howdy there, John!" he exclaimed. "Glad ya finally done brought yourself on in here! These here boys-a yours ain't been none too friendly."

John Wallace looked solemnly at Mr. Tom Bee. "What ya want, Tom?"

"Wants me my sardines and some candy there, John."

Dewberry slammed his fist hard upon the counter. "Daddy! How come you to let this old nigger disrespect ya this here way? Just lettin' him stand there and talk to you like he was a white man! He need teachin', Daddy! He need teachin'!"

"Dew's right," said Thurston. "Them old britches done stretched way too big!"

John Wallace wheeled around and fixed hard, unrelenting eyes on his sons. "Y'all hush up and get on to ya business! There's stackin' to be done out back!"

"But, Daddy—"

"I said get!"

For a moment Dewberry and Thurston didn't move. The heat seemed more stifling. The quiet more quiet. John

Wallace kept eyes on his sons. Dewberry and Thurston left the store.

As the back door closed behind them Stacey went in and got Christopher-John. Mr. John Wallace took note of him, took note of all of us, and as Stacey and Christopher-John came out he came behind and closed the doors. But he forgot the open windows. He turned back to Mr. Tom Bee. "Now, Tom," he said, "I done told you before 'bout calling me by my Christian name, it ain't jus' the two of us. It ain't seemly, you here a nigger and me a white man. Now you ain't used to do it. Some folks say it's yo' old age. Say your age is making you forget 'bout way things is. But I say it ain't your age, it's your orneriness."

Mr. Tom Bee squared his shoulders. "An' I done tole you, it ain't seemly t' me to be callin' no white man mister when I done saved his sorry hide when he wasn't hardly no older'n them younguns standin' out yonder! You owes me, John. Ya knows ya owes me too."

John Wallace walked back to the counter. "Ain't necessarily what I'm wanting, but what's gotta be. You just can't keep going 'round callin' me by my first name no more. Folks been taking note. Makes me look bad. Even my boys been questionin' me on why I lets ya do it."

"Then tell 'em, doggonit!"

"I'm losin' face, Tom."

"Now, what you think I care 'bout your face, boy? I done saved your hide more'n one time and I gots me a right t' call you whatsoever I pleases t' call you whensoever I be talkin' t' ya!"

John Wallace sucked in his breath. "Naw, Tom, not no more."

Mr. Tom Bee sucked in his breath too. "You figure the years done made you forget how come you alive an' still breathin'?"

"Figure the years done give me sense 'bout this thing."

"Well, you live long 'nough, maybe the next years gonna give you the sense 'nough t' be grateful. Now put these here sardines on my charges." He glanced over at the candy jars. "An' give me two pennies worth-a them there candy sticks while's you at it."

Mr. Tom Bee stood quietly waiting as if expecting his order to be obeyed, and to our surprise Mr. John Wallace did obey. He reached into the candy jar, pulled out a fistful of candy canes, and handed them to him. Mr. Tom Bee took the candy canes and gave John Wallace a nod. Mr. John Wallace put both hands flat on the counter.

"Tom, mind what I say now. My patience done worn thin 'bout 'mindin' you 'bout what's proper. Next time you come in here, you make sure you address me right, you hear?"

Mr. Tom Bee cackled a laugh and slapped one string of fish on the counter. "These here for you, John. Knows how much you like catfish, so these here for you!" Then, still chuckling, he picked up his cans of sardines and stuffed them into his pockets, turned his back on John Wallace, and left the store.

As soon as Mr. Tom Bee was outside, he looked down at Christopher-John and said, "How'd y'all younguns like a little bit-a candy?"

"Like it just fine, Mr. Tom Bee!" spoke up Christopher-John.

Mr. Tom Bee laughed and handed him a stick, then presented one each to Stacey, Little Man, and me. Stacey, Christopher-John, and I were mighty thankful, but Little Man only looked joylessly at his candy cane and stuck it into his shirt pocket.

"What's this?" asked Mr. Tom Bee. "What's this? Ain't ya gonna eat that candy cane, boy?"

Little Man shook his head.

"Well, why not? Mighty good!"

"Don't want they ole candy canes! They said I was dirty! I ain't dirty, Mr. Tom Bee!"

Mr. Tom Bee put his hands on his hips and laughed. "Lord have mercy! Course ya ain't, boy! Don't you know them Wallace boys ain't got no more good sense'n a wall-eyed mule! Last thing in the world ya wantin' to be doin' is listenin' to anything they gotta say! They say somethin's red, ya best be figurin' it's green. They say somethin' dirty, ya gotta know it's clean! Shuckies, Little Man! You got more sense with them six years a your'n than them two boys ever gonna see. Don't ya never pay them no mind!"

Little Man thought on that, looked around at Stacey, who nodded his agreement with Mr. Tom Bee, then took the candy cane from his pocket and gave it a listless lick.

Then Mr. Tom Bee noticed Jeremy and snapped, "You the kinda boy keep hold to yo' promises?"

Jeremy, who seemed taken aback by the question, nodded mutely.

At that, Mr. Tom Bee pulled forth another candy cane and held it out to him. The boys and I waited, wondering if Jeremy would take it. Jeremy seemed to be wondering if he should. He hesitated, looked around as if fearful someone other than we would see, and took it. He didn't actually say thank you to Mr. Tom Bee, but then the nod he gave and his eyes did. I had a feeling Jeremy didn't see much penny candy either.

As Mr. Tom Bee, the boys, and I started down the road, Jeremy called after us. "Stacey! May—maybe one-a these here days, maybe I go fishin' with y'all. . . . "

"Yeah. . . . " Stacey replied. "Yeah, one-a these days, maybe so. . . . "

We headed on toward Aunt Callie's. Stacey sucked thoughtfully at his candy stick, then looked up at Mr. Tom Bee. "Mr. Tom Bee, something I been thinkin' on."

"What's that, boy?"

" 'Bout how come you to call Mr. Wallace plain-out by his first name. I mean you don't call him mister or nothin'." He paused. "Don't know nobody else to do, nobody colored I mean. Fact to business, don't know nobody colored call a white man straight to his face by his first name."

Mr. Tom Bee laughed. "He call me straight-out Tom 'thout no mister, don't he now?"

Stacey nodded. "Yes, sir, that's a fact, but that's the way white folks do. Papa say white folks set an awful store 'bout names and such. He say they get awful riled 'bout them names too. Say they can do some terrible things when they get riled. Say anybody call a white man straight out by his name just lookin' for trouble."

"Well, that's sho the truth all right," agreed Mr. Tom Bee. "But shuckies! I ain't studyin' they foolish way-a things and I ain't gonna be callin' that John Wallace no mister neither! He done promised me long time ago I could call him straight out by his name long's I lived an' I aims to see he holds to his promises." He paused, then added, " 'Sides, we used t' be friends."

"Friends?" said Stacey as if he didn't understand the word.

"That's right. Me and that John Wallace, we goes way back. Long ways back. Why, shuckies! I done saved that boy's life!"

We all looked up from our candy canes.

"That's right!" he said with an emphatic nod. "Sho did! That John Wallace wasn't no more'n fifteen when I come along the road one day and found him sinkin' in swampland and pulled him out. Asked him what his name was. He said, call me John. So's that what I called him, jus' that. John. But that there was only the first time I done saved his life.

"No sooner'n I done got him outa that swampland, I come t' find out he was burnin' up with fever, so's I doctored him. Ain't never laid eyes on the boy before, but I doctored him anyways. Doctored him till I got him well. Turned out the boy ain't had no family round here. Said he was coming up from down Biloxi way when he landed hisself in that swamp. Anyways, I let him stay on with me till he got hisself strong. Let him stay on long's he wanted and that was for quite some while, till the white folks round started meddlin' 'bout a white boy stayin' wit' me. I done took care-a John Wallace like a daddy woulda and long's he stayed with me, he minded what I said and was right respectful."

Stacey shook his head as if finding that hard to believe.

Mr. Tom Bee saw the disbelief and assured him it was so. "That's right! Right respectful, and all that time, I been callin' him John. Jus' that. John. Well, come the day John Wallace tole me he was goin' up to Vicksburg to look for a job an' I said to him I figured next time I see him, I 'spected I'd most likely hafta be callin' him *Mister* John. And he told me things wasn't never gonna be that way. He says to me, I'm John t' you now, gonna always be John t' ya, cause you been like a daddy t' me an' I couldn't never 'spect

my daddy to go callin' me mister. He done promised me that. Promised me he wasn't never gonna forget what I done for him. Said he was gonna always owe me. But then he come back down in here some years later to set up that store and things had done changed. He 'spected all the colored folks to call him 'Mister' John, and that there done included ole Tom Bee."

"Owww," I said, "Mr. John Wallace done broke his word!"

"He sho done that all right! Now I been thinkin' here lately maybe it's time I makes him keep his word. I figures I'm close 'nough to meetin' my Maker, it don't much matter he like it or not. I ain't studyin' that boy!"

I took a lick of candy. "Well, Big Ma—she say you gonna get yourself in a whole lotta trouble, Mr. Tom Bee. She say all them years on you done made you go foolish—"

"Cassie!" Stacey rebuked me with a hard look.

I gave him a look right back. "Well, she did!" Not only had Big Ma said it, but plenty of other folks had too. They said Mr. Tom Bee had just all of a sudden up and started calling Mr. Wallace John. He had started after years of addressing John Wallace like the white folks expected him to do. Most folks figured the only reason for him to do a fool thing like that was because he had gone forgetful, that his advancing years were making him think it was a long time back when John Wallace was still a boy. I told it all. "Said you just full of foolishness callin' that man by his name that way!"

Mr. Tom Bee stopped right in the middle of the road, slapped his thighs, and let go a rip of a laugh. "Well, ya know somethin', Cassie? Maybe yo' grandmama's right! Jus' maybe she sho is! Maybe I done gone foolish! Jus' maybe I has!"

He laughed so hard standing there, I thought he was going to cry. But then after a few moments he started walking again and the boys and I got right into step. Still chuckling, Mr. Tom Bee said he couldn't rightly say he hadn't been called foolish before. In fact, he said, he'd been called foolish more times than he wanted to remember. Then he began to tell us about one of those times, and the boys and I listened eagerly. We loved to hear Mr. Tom Bee tell his stories. With all his years, he had plenty of stories to tell too. He had seen the slavery days and he had seen the war that ended slavery. He had seen Confederate soldiers and he had seen Yankee soldiers. He had seen a lot of things over the years and he said he'd forgotten just about as much as he remembered. But as we walked the road listening to him I for one was mighty glad he had remembered as much as he had.

We reached Aunt Callie's, gave her the head medicine and the fish, then headed back toward home. Mr. Tom Bee was still with us. He lived over our way. To get home we had to pass the Wallace store again. When we reached the crossroads, Mr. Tom Bee said, "Y'all wait on up jus' another minute here. Done forgot my tobaccie." A truck and a wagon were now in front of the store. Mr. Tom Bee took note of them and stepped onto the porch.

Jeremy Simms was still sitting on the porch, but he didn't say anything to us this time. He nodded slightly, that was all. I noticed he wasn't sucking on his candy cane; I could

see it sticking out of his pocket. He bit his lip and looked around uneasily. We didn't say anything to him either. We just stood there wanting to get on home. It was getting late.

Mr. Tom Bee entered the store. " 'Ey there, John!" he called. "Give me some-a that chewin' tobaccie! Forgot to get it I was in before."

The boys and I, standing by the gas pump, looked into the store. So did Jeremy. His father, Mr. Charlie Simms, was in there now, sitting at the table by the stove along with his older teenage brothers, R.W. and Melvin. Dewberry and Thurston Wallace were there also and two white men we didn't know. They all turned their eyes on Mr. Tom Bee. Dewberry and Thurston glanced at their father, and then Mr. Charlie Simms spoke up. "Old nigger," he said, "who you think you talkin' to?"

Mr. Tom Bee wet his lips. "Jus' . . . jus' come for my tobaccie."

Mr. John Wallace glanced at the men, then, his jaw hardening, set eyes on Mr. Tom Bee. "You bes' get on outa here, Tom."

Mr. Tom Bee looked around at the men. His back straightened with that old, sharp-edged stubbornness. "Well, I sho do that, John," he said, "soon's I get me my tobaccie."

Mr. Simms jumped up from the table. "John Wallace! You jus' gonna let this here old nigger talk t' ya this-a way? You gon' let him do that?"

Suddenly Stacey bounded up the steps to the store entrance. "We—we waitin' on ya, Mr. Tom Bee!" he cried shrilly. "We waitin'! Come on, Mr. Tom Bee! Come on!"

Mr. Tom Bee looked over at him. He took a moment, then he nodded and I thought he was going to come on out. But instead he said, "Be right wit' ya, boy . . . soon's I get me my tobaccie." Then he turned again and faced John Wallace. "You—you gonna give me that tobaccie, John?"

Dewberry pulled from the counter. "Daddy! You don't shut this old nigger up, I'm gonna do it for ya!"

Mr. John Wallace turned a mean look on his son and the look was enough to silence him. Then he looked around

the room at Mr. Simms, at R.W. and Melvin, at Thurston, at the two other white men gathered there. The store and all around it was plunged into silence.

Mr. Tom Bee glanced nervously at the men, but he didn't stop. He seemed bent on carrying this thing through. "Well?" he asked of John Wallace. "I'm gonna get me that tobaccie?"

Silently John Wallace reached back to a shelf and got the tobacco. He placed it on the counter.

Mr. Simms exploded. "What kind-a white man are ya, John Wallace, ya don't shut his black mouth? What kind-a white man?"

Mr. Tom Bee looked at Mr. Simms and the others, then went and picked up the tobacco. "Thank ya, John," he said. "Jus' put it on my charges there, John. Jus' put it on my charges." He glanced again at the men and started out. He got as far as the steps. The boys and I turned to go. Then we heard the click. The explosion of a shotgun followed and Mr. Tom Bee tumbled down the steps, his right leg ripped open by the blast.

The boys and I stood stunned, just staring at Mr. Tom Bee at first, not knowing what to do. Stacey started toward him, but Mr. Tom Bee waved him back. "Get 'way from me, boy! Get 'way! Stacey, get them younguns back, 'way from me!" Stacey looked into the store, at the shotgun, and herded us across the road.

The white men came out and sniggered. Mr. John Wallace, carrying the shotgun, came out onto the porch too. He stood there, his face solemn, and said, "You made me do that, Tom. I coulda killed ya, but I ain't wantin' to kill ya 'cause ya done saved my life an' I'm a Christian man so I ain't forgetting that. But this here disrespectin' me gotta stop and I means to stop it now. You gotta keep in mind you ain't nothin' but a nigger. You gonna learn to watch yo' mouth. You gonna learn to address me proper. You hear me, Tom?"

Mr. Tom Bee sat in silence staring at the bloody leg.

"Tom, ya hear me?"

Now, slowly, Mr. Tom Bee raised his head and looked up at John Wallace. "Oh, yeah, I hears ya all right. I hears

ya. But let me tell you somethin', John. Ya was John t' me when I saved your sorry life and you give me your word you was always gonna be John t' me long as I lived. So's ya might's well go 'head and kill me cause that's what ya gon' be, John. Ya hear me, John? Till the judgment day. Till the earth opens itself up and the fires-a hell come takes yo' ungrateful soul! Ya hear me, John? Ya hear me? *John! John! John!* Till the judgment day! *John!*"

With that he raised himself to one elbow and began to drag himself down the road. The boys and I, candy canes in hand, stood motionless. We watched Mr. John Wallace to see if he would raise the shotgun again. Jeremy, the candy cane in his pocket, watched too. We all waited for the second click of the shotgun. But only the cries of Mr. Tom Bee as he inched his way along the road ripped the silence. "*John! John! John!*" he cried over and over again. "Ya hear me, John? Till the judgment day! John! *John! JOHN!*"

There was no other sound.

Author's Note

I was born in the South but I didn't grow up there. In fact, I was only three months old when my parents took my sister and me to live in the North. Over the years of my childhood I came to know the South through the yearly trips my family took to Mississippi and through the stories told whenever the family gathered, both in the North and in the South. Through the stories I learned a history about my family going back to the days of slavery. Through the stories I learned a history not then taught in history books, a history about the often tragic lives of Black people living in a segregated land. My father told many of the stories. Some of the stories he had been told when he was a boy. Some of the stories he actually lived himself. *The Friendship* is based on one of those stories.

Mildred D. Taylor was born in Jackson, Mississippi, and grew up in Toledo, Ohio. After graduating from the University of Toledo, she spent two years in Ethiopia with the Peace Corps. Returning to the United States, she entered the School of Journalism at the University of Colorado, where she worked with students and university officials in structuring a Black Studies program at the university.

Mildred Taylor's first book about the Logan family, *Song of the Trees* (Dial), won the Council on Interracial Books Award in the African American Category. She won the 1977 Newbery Medal for *Roll of Thunder, Hear My Cry*, and the Coretta Scott King Award for each of her later books about the Logan family, *Let the Circle Be Unbroken*, *The Road to Memphis*, and *The Friendship* (all Dial and Puffin). She lives in Boulder, Colorado.

Max Ginsburg has exhibited his paintings in many one-man shows, and has also created book covers and magazine illustrations. He has received a number of awards, including the Gold Medal from the Society of Illustrators. Mr. Ginsburg received his bachelor of fine arts degree from Syracuse University and his master of arts from the City College of New York. In addition to painting, he also teaches art in New York City, where he lives.